SHONEN JUMP'S Yu-Gi-Oh! GX ™

Adapted by Tracey West

I CHALLENGE YOU!

SCHOLASTIC INC.

New York   Toronto   London   Auckland   Sydney
Mexico City   New Delhi   Hong Kong   Buenos Aires

ISBN 0-439-88839-5

©1996 Kazuki Takahashi
©2004 NAS•TV TOKYO

Published by Scholastic Inc.
SCHOLASTIC and associated logos are trademarks and/or registered trademarks of Scholastic Inc.

12 11 10 9 8 7 6 5 4 3 2 1   6 7 8 9 10 11/0

Printed in the U.S.A.
First printing, November 2006

Jaden Yuki stood on the pitcher's mound.

Bastion, another student at Duel Academy, was at bat.

"You're going down!" Jaden called out.

Nearby, Dr. Crowler talked to himself.

"I need to find someone who can beat Jaden!" he said.

Then, bam! Bastion hit the ball. It hit Dr. Crowler in the eye!

Dr. Crowler was mad. But then he saw
Bastion.

Dr. Crowler had an idea.

Dr. Crowler began the first step of his plan.

"Tomorrow you will duel Bastion," Crowler told Chazz. "If you lose to him, you two will switch dorms."

Chazz was not happy. He liked being in Obelisk, the top dorm.

"I won't be a Ra Yellow!" he cried.

After the game, Jaden and Syrus talked to Bastion.

"I play like I duel – with formulas," Bastion said.

"Do you have a formula for everything, Bastion?" Syrus asked.

Bastion showed Jaden and Syrus his dorm room. He had formulas written on every wall.

Bastion had no more room to write on his walls.

Jaden and Syrus helped him paint the room.

It got kind of messy, but they all had fun.

Chazz looked out of his window.

"Bastion is heading off to the Slifer dorm for the night," he said. "Hmm. Then his dorm room will be all empty."

That gave Chazz an idea of his own.

The next morning, Miss Dorothy knocked on Jaden's door.

"I was at the docks," she said. "Then I saw them. Cards tossed everywhere!"

The boys rushed to the docks.

Bastion's Duel Monsters cards floated in the water!

"This was your deck and it's totally ruined!" Jaden cried. "Your promotion exam is in less than an hour."

Bastion had no choice. He went to the battle arena.

Zane and Alexis, two Obelisk students, were there.

"I saw you, Chazz," Alexis said. "This morning by the water."

"Who's to say I wasn't throwing away my own cards?" Chazz said.

Jaden knew Chazz was lying. But Bastion was not worried.

"You saw all of my different formulas," he said. "They were for all my different dueling decks!"

Bastion and Chazz began the duel with 4000 life points each.

"I summon Cthonian Soldier!" Chazz
cried. "Then a card facedown."

"Rise, Hydrogeddon!" Bastion called out. "With Hydrogust – destroy him!"

Bam! Hydrogeddon blasted Chazz's monster with a powerful gust of wind.

Chazz's life points dropped to 3600.

"Thanks," Chazz said. "You just activated my Cthonian Soldier's special ability. It causes you to take the same amount of damage to your life points that I did."

Bastion's life points dropped to 3600, too.

Bastion's card had a special ability, too. He summoned another Hydrogeddon from his deck.

Chazz's life points dropped to 2000.

"You'll pay for that!" Chazz cried.

Chazz activated a trap card. He used Call of the Haunted to summon Cthonian Soldier from his graveyard.

Then Chazz used Infernal Reckless Summon.

"It allows us both to summon in attack mode any monsters in the deck or grave-yard that are the same as monsters we have on the field," he explained.

Now each duelist had three monsters on the field.

Then Chazz used a spell card, Cthonian Alliance. His first Cthonian Soldier gained 800 points for every soldier on the field.

Now Chazz's first monster had a massive 3600 attack points!

"Attack, Cthonian Soldier!" Chazz yelled.

The Cthonian Soldier took out one of the Hydrogeddons. Bastion's life points dropped to 1600.

Bastion called on Oxygeddon. The dragon-like monster took out two of the Cthonian Soldiers with Vapor String.

"That damage is still going back to you, loser!" Chazz said.

Chazz was right. Chazz's life points dropped to 1000. And Bastion's life points dropped to 600. He took damage every time he destroyed a Cthonian Soldier.

"Oh man, why does Bastion keep attacking?" Syrus asked. "He's only hurting himself."

"Nah, he's fine," Jaden said.

Syrus looked at the stats. Jaden was right.

The big Cthonian Soldier lost attack points every time another soldier was destroyed. Now its attack points were back down to 2000.

"Now I'll play a facedown card, and that'll do for now," Bastion said.

"Will it? I'm not so sure, whiz kid!" Chazz said.

"I am sacrificing Cthonian Soldier and all the cards in my hand to summon Infernal Incinerator," Chazz said.

Infernal Incinerator had 2800 attack points. But the monster got 200 extra points for every monster on the field. It towered over the field with 3400 attack points!

"If you can't find a formula to beat this guy, you're toast!" Chazz yelled. "Infernal Incinerator, attack with Fire Storm Blast!"

A wall of blazing hot fire streamed from the monster. But Bastion activated a trap.

"I activate Amorphic Barrier!" he cried.

Because Bastion had three monsters on the field, the barrier stopped the attack.

"So what?" Chazz asked. "One turn. That's all it buys you."

"I'm afraid there won't be a next turn," Bastion said.

Chazz was shocked. "What?"

Bastion used the spell card Bonding H$_2$O. He sacrificed his monsters to summon Water Dragon.

Water Dragon attacked Infernal Incinerator with a huge tidal wave. The water blast took down the monster. His attack points dropped to 0.

"That is Water Dragon's special ability," Bastion explained. "When he's out on the field, the attack points of fire and pyro types become zero."

A wave of water knocked Chazz down. His life points dropped to zero.

Dr. Crowler was happy. He told Bastion he could go to the Obelisk dorm.

"No," Bastion said. "I decided I would only enter Obelisk Blue when I become the number one student in freshman class. Jaden, I think that student is you."

"Thanks!" Jaden said. "Does that mean you want to settle this right here?"

"Sorry, but not now," Bastion said. "I have a lot of work to do before I duel you."

Jaden nodded.

When Bastion wanted to duel, he would be ready!